The Witch and the Ring

by Ruth Chew

Illustrations by the author

A
LITTLE **APPLE**
PAPERBACK

SCHOLASTIC INC.

New York Toronto London Auckland Sydney

ISBN 0-590-42056-9

12 11 10 9 8 7 6 5 4 0 1 2 3 4/9

Printed in the U.S.A. 28

First Scholastic Printing, March 1989

To Betty and Bernard Chew

1

"CHARLOTTE, I heard a hen cackle!" Walt Foley grabbed his sister's arm.

Charlotte looked around the busy street corner. "Don't be silly. People don't keep chickens at the corner of McDonald and Church!"

It was always noisy here in the afternoon. Car radios blasted. Children rode bicycles and skateboards. Mothers pushed babies in strollers. And people stood on the sidewalk and talked to their friends.

Mixed in with all the noise, Charlotte *did* hear the clucking of a hen. She looked around and saw a small gray-haired woman holding out pamphlets.

"Cluck, cluck." There was that cackling again! It certainly wasn't coming from the old woman.

Walt pointed to a little girl bouncing up and down on a "kangaroo" ride in front of a store.

Next to the moving kangaroo was a big yellow plastic box. It had a steep orange roof and windows on each side. Inside the box a life-sized plastic hen sat on a pile of bright-colored eggs.

Walt ran over to the box. "The clucking is coming from this fake chicken!"

Charlotte looked at the sign on top of the orange roof:

FUN CHICKEN

There were pictures on the box — a top, a ring, a string of beads, an airplane.

Walt saw a smaller sign:

Lottery Tickets, Watches in LUCKY eggs
Two prizes in gold eggs!

"I need a watch." Walt took a coin out of his pocket.

PUSH IN. PULL OUT.

was written over a slot like those in the laundromat. And there was another sign:

INSERT ONE QUARTER ONLY

"Charlotte," Walt said, "I only have a dime."

"I bought colored pencils with my allowance," Charlotte told him.

Something rolled across the sidewalk and bumped into Walt's left shoe.

"Clink!" It fell over and lay on its side.

Walt picked it up. "Guess what! Here's a quarter!"

Charlotte and Walt went to all the people on the corner to ask if they'd dropped a quarter. At last they walked over to the little old woman with the pamphlets.

"Excuse me," Charlotte said. "Did you lose a quarter?"

"Certainly not!" a harsh voice snapped. The woman glared at Charlotte. Her green eyes flashed under her shaggy eyebrows.

Charlotte stepped back so suddenly she almost fell over Walt.

"I guess I can use the quarter." Walt ran back to the Fun Chicken and put the quarter into the slot.

2

THE plastic chicken cackled. It began turning around and around.

Plop! An egg dropped into a little box near the bottom of the chicken house.

Walt bent down. "It's not a gold egg, so we won't get two prizes." He picked up an orange and blue plastic egg and pulled it apart at the crack in the middle.

Walt looked inside. "Empty! This whole thing is a gyp!" He started to throw the egg on the ground.

"Don't litter!" Charlotte ran over to take the two halves of the plastic egg.

A scraggly little gray cat crouching near Walt's feet jumped out of the way.

"Oh," Charlotte said to the cat. "Where did you come from? I almost stepped on you!"

She held half the egg in each hand. "That's funny. The blue half is heavier!" Charlotte poked her finger into the shell and pulled out a very small blue ring.

Walt looked hard at it. "That's not big enough for either of us."

"But isn't it pretty!" Charlotte said. "Kind of like a starry sky."

The entire ring was a deep blue with little silvery flecks in it that twinkled in the afternoon sunlight. It felt cool in Charlotte's hand.

"What's it made of?" Walt asked.

"I don't know," his sister answered.

"Give it to me, Charlotte." Walt reached for the ring.

Charlotte pretended to put the tiny ring on his finger. To her surprise, it went right on. A shiver ran down Charlotte's back. She was sure the ring had been much too small for Walt only a minute ago.

"It fits just as if it was made for me," Walt said. "But it makes my finger feel hot. Anyway, this isn't a boy's ring." He handed it back to her.

Charlotte was older than her brother. Her hands were bigger. She thought hard. Then Charlotte slipped the ring on her *thumb!*

Charlotte and Walt just stared at the ring. Neither of them could say a word.

Charlotte swallowed hard. Then she whispered, "Did you see that?"

Walt nodded. "Spooky! We'd better get rid of it."

Charlotte took the ring off her thumb. It was magic and probably dangerous. Maybe Walt was right. But the ring was so beautiful that she couldn't bear to give it up.

"MEOW!" It was such a loud cry that Charlotte almost dropped the ring!

She looked down to see the scraggly little gray cat. Charlotte leaned over to stroke it. The cat jumped back.

"Don't worry. I won't hurt you," Charlotte said. "Come on, Walt. Let's go home. Mother will wonder what's happened to us." She slipped the ring back on her thumb and started walking fast.

3

As they were going home on Church Avenue, Charlotte began to walk so fast that Walt had to run to keep up with her. "Why the big hurry, Charlotte?"

"I have a feeling somebody is following us," his sister told him.

"That's silly!" Walt said.

Charlotte knew her brother was right. She was being silly, but still she had that prickly feeling on the back of her neck. She turned around to look behind her.

Half a block away there was a woman all dressed in black. Charlotte saw her duck out of sight into a doorway.

Now Charlotte started walking very slowly. She bent over to tie a shoelace and peeked through her legs. There was the woman in black again! She was still a half block away. Charlotte strained her eyes to see better. The woman seemed to have a sharp nose and chin and shaggy gray hair.

Charlotte stood up straight again. "Walt," she said, "there *is* somebody following us. It's a lady dressed in black." Charlotte started to walk faster.

After a moment or two Walt took a look behind him. A second later he yelled, "Run, Charlotte!" and took off down the street.

Charlotte raced after him.

After they crossed the next street, Walt whispered, "Charlotte, that was the nasty woman with the pamphlets."

Charlotte looked back down Church Avenue. "Where is she now?"

"That's the scary part," Walt said. "I never took my eyes off her, but all at once she was gone. She must be a witch! Charlotte, you'd better get rid of that ring!"

The beautiful blue ring on Charlotte's thumb started to sparkle. Charlotte thought it was smiling at her. "I just want to keep the ring a little while," she said. "This might be my only chance to get mixed up with magic."

The children turned the corner onto the street where they lived. Their mother was waiting for them on the front stoop of their house. Walt and Charlotte ran up the steps.

Mrs. Foley gave each of them a hug. She looked down. "And who is this?"

The scraggly little gray cat was sitting on the top step, looking up at their mother with bright green eyes.

Walt started at the skinny cat. "She must have followed us all the way home from McDonald Avenue, Mom."

"Poor thing!" Mrs. Foley said. "I've never seen such hungry eyes." She stretched out her hand to pet the cat.

At once it moved out of reach.

"If she's still around after supper, I'll put out some leftovers for her. Now come into the house. Your dad will be home soon." Mrs. Foley opened the front door.

Before Charlotte had her foot in the doorway, the cat streaked past her into the house.

4

"THE cat doesn't want to wait till after supper. Don't worry, Mom. I'll get her out of here." Walt ran into the house after the cat.

While Mrs. Foley cooked supper, Charlotte set the table in the dining room.

Walt came down from upstairs. "She's not in the bedrooms." He raced through the house and went down the basement steps.

When Charlotte heard her father open the front door, she ran to greet him.

Mr. Foley gave her a kiss and handed her his jacket. "M-m-m! I smell corned-beef hash."

Charlotte hung her father's jacket in the hall closet.

Mr. Foley walked into the kitchen. "Where's Walt?"

"He's looking for a cat that sneaked into the house." Mrs. Foley went to the head of the basement stairs and called down, "Walt, Daddy's home."

Walt came puffing up the stairs. "I found the cat, but I can't get to her. She's up on some water pipes over the furnace." He grinned. "I shut the furnace room door. At least I know where she is."

"Never a dull moment around here," Mr. Foley said.

Midway through supper Mr. Foley asked, "What's that on Charlotte's thumb?"

"A magic ring," Walt told him. "It changes size."

Mr. and Mrs. Foley looked at each other and smiled. Then Mr. Foley said, "May I see it, Charlotte? Please."

Until now, the ring had been cool against Charlotte's skin. Suddenly it was hot, and getting hotter every second!

Charlotte pulled it off her thumb.

Her father reached out and took the magic ring.

The ring had been so hot that Charlotte expected her father to drop it at once. Instead he held in in the palm of his hand and even squeezed it.

Mrs. Foley leaned over to take a look. "I once had a ring with a split in the back like this one," she said. "They can fit anybody. What's it made of?"

"Soft plastic," her husband told her. "Where'd you get the ring, Charlotte?"

"Walt got it from a Fun Chicken egg," Charlotte said. "He wanted a watch."

Mr. Foley laughed. "I've seen that thing you're talking about, on the corner near the bank. But I never yet saw

anybody find a watch in one of those eggs. Do you think you can wait till your birthday, son?"

Walt grinned. "Sure can!"

Mr. Foley handed the ring back to Charlotte. It felt cool and hard, with no sign of a break in the back. Charlotte put it on the middle finger of her left hand and went on eating her supper.

5

WHEN it was time for dessert, Mrs. Foley said, "Dad and I have to do some shopping, children. The stores close at nine. We'd better go now. Get yourselves ice-cream pops from the freezer. And please put the supper dishes into the dishwasher. I'll turn it on when I come home."

Walt cleared the dirty plates while Charlotte stood on a kitchen chair to reach into the freezer top of the refrigerator.

They heard the front door bang as their mother and father went out.

The two children ate the ice-cream pops at the kitchen table.

When they were finished, Walt said, "Charlotte, why didn't we notice the break in the back of the ring?"

His sister gave him the ring. Walt

looked at it all over. The ring was just as hard and smooth as when they had first seen it. The little silvery flecks shone softly in the complete blue circle.

"It's much too hot to handle! How can you stand to wear it, Charlotte?" Walt handed the ring back to her.

"MEOW!"

The gray cat was sitting in the middle of the kitchen floor looking at Walt and Charlotte with her bright green eyes.

Walt stared at the cat. "How did you get out of the furnace room?"

The cat opened her pink mouth and yawned.

"Oh, that's right," Charlotte stood up. "Mother said she was going to put out some leftovers for you. I see there's some corned-beef hash on her plate."

Charlotte looked in her mother's catch-all drawer and took out a blue plastic lid that had once belonged to a little tub of ice cream. "Here's a dish for you, little cat!" Charlotte put the leftover hash in the lid.

Walt took a crumpled paper napkin off his plate. A mound of peas and carrots had been hiding under the napkin. "I wonder if she'd like these." Walt scraped the vegetables into the plastic lid.

Charlotte put the lid on the floor near the gray cat. The cat looked first at the food and then at the children.

"It's okay, cat," Walt said. "You can eat it."

Charlotte bent down to stroke her. At once the cat ran under the kitchen table.

"Don't be afraid. Nobody's going to hurt you." Charlotte put the blue plastic lid under the table. "Is that better?"

The cat waited until both Walt and Charlotte were on the other side of the kitchen before she started to eat.

6

"No wonder this cat doesn't like us," Charlotte said. "We keep calling her *cat*. I wonder if she has a name."

"I just had an idea," Walt said. "Do you remember Dad's story about those people who couldn't think of the right name for their baby?"

Charlotte thought for a minute. "Didn't they wait till she was learning to talk and then read lists of names to her?"

Walt nodded. "Then one day the baby's mother saw her standing in front of the mirror pointing to herself and saying, 'Ba Ba!' "

"So they named the baby Barbara,"

Charlotte remembered. "But what does that have to do with the cat? She can't point to herself and say 'Smoky' or whatever her name is."

"I don't think cats are as smart as dogs," Walt said, "but they answer to their names."

"It's worth a try." Charlotte lay on her stomach so she could look at the cat. She recited all the cat names she could think of. The cat went on eating.

Then Walt took his turn. He had no luck, either.

Somehow names like Frisky and Whiskers didn't seem to fit the cat.

When she had eaten everything in the plastic lid, the cat crouched in the shadows under the table, with her ears cocked. Her eyes were like two green lights, watching the children.

"Maybe she doesn't have a cat name." Charlotte stood up and went to get the

dog-eared old dictionary from the living room bookcase. She turned to the list of first names.

"Abigail, Ada, Adela," Charlotte read.

The cat closed her eyes and looked bored.

But Charlotte began to enjoy this. There were such wonderful names, and most of them had meanings. Alice meant truth; Amanda, lovable.

Walt kept his eyes on the cat. When Charlotte read, "Arabella, meaning and origin uncertain," the end of the cat's scraggly tail twitched.

"Charlotte," Walt said, "try that one again."

"Arabella," Charlotte repeated.

This time the cat laid her ears back. Her tail stopped twitching.

Charlotte studied the book. "The French say, 'Arabelle.' Perhaps her name is Arabelle! Is that your name? Arabelle?" Charlotte said.

The cat stood up and stretched.

"I don't like it when people get my name wrong, either," Charlotte said. "What else would you like to eat, Arabelle?"

The cat came out from under the table, but she stayed as far from the children as possible without leaving the kitchen.

7

"ARABELLE is afraid of us, Walt," Charlotte said. "She doesn't seem to want to be with people. Maybe she never belonged to anybody before."

Walt thought about this. "Some kids do mean things to cats." He crawled under the table to get the plastic lid.

Walt spread peanut butter on a cracker and put it in the lid. "Mom's not crazy about crumbs all over the place, Arabelle." He put the blue lid on the floor.

The cat wouldn't go near it until Walt moved away.

Walt looked at the clock. "It's after eight-thirty. Mom and Dad will be home soon." He opened the dishwasher and started putting the dirty dishes into it.

When Charlotte picked up the four

dinner plates, they slid right out of her hands.

"Now you've done it!" Walt said.

But instead of crashing to the ground, the plates floated over to stack themselves neatly in the dishwasher.

Charlotte was so surprised that she knocked a saucer off the sink top. It gave a little shake and tucked itself safely into the dishwasher, too.

Charlotte felt the ring on her finger move! She saw that it was turning like a wheel and sparkling. "Walt!" she whispered, "The ring is magicking the plates!"

"That looks like fun," Walt said.

"Why don't you try it?" Charlotte handed the ring to her brother.

Walt put it on his right hand. "Funny," he said. "It doesn't feel hot to me now."

The cat was crunching away at the cracker. She hadn't noticed what was going on. Now she was trying to lick a lump of peanut butter off her nose.

Arabelle ate every scrap before she washed her face and combed her whiskers. Then she looked around.

Walt was standing across the room from the dishwasher. He was throwing the knives, forks, and spoons like darts. They flew right to the silverware basket in the dishwasher.

The last thing to go in was the big serving platter. Charlotte took the ring from Walt. She was taking no chances with this dish.

Arabelle had finished her supper now. When the cat saw Charlotte pick up the

platter, she gave a leap and knocked it out of her hands.

The ring spun around on Charlotte's finger and shot sparks like a firecracker.

Clunk! The platter banged Arabelle on the nose, sailed around the room, and coasted down into the dishwasher.

Arabelle let out a yowl.

"Serves you right, cat!" Walt said. "Why did you try to smash Mom's big platter?"

"She saw us playing with the dishes and wanted to have fun, too," Charlotte told him. She went over to pet the cat. Before Charlotte could touch her, Arabelle ran under the kitchen table. She huddled back against the wall.

"Come on out, Arabelle," Charlotte said. "I'm sorry you got hurt. But it's lucky you didn't break the plate. I want Mother to like you. Maybe she'll let you live here."

8

THE front door opened. Mr. and Mrs. Foley walked into the house. They were both carrying sacks of groceries.

Charlotte ran to help carry the bags to the kitchen.

"You have to meet Arabelle, Dad," Walt said.

"Who is Arabelle?" Mr. Foley asked.

"The cat," Walt told him.

"Did you let her out of the furnace room?" his father wanted to know.

"She let herself out," Charlotte said.

"Smart cat!" Mr. Foley started unpacking the groceries.

"Why do you call her Arabelle?" Mrs. Foley asked.

"She said that was her name." Charlotte stooped to look under the table. "She's down here, Mother."

Mrs. Foley bent down to see.

Arabelle was hunched into a sad little ball of gray fur. "Has she had anything to eat?" Mrs. Foley asked.

"Yes," Walt said. "We gave her everything left on the supper plates, and then some!"

Mrs. Foley was sure the cat had not had enough. But Arabelle wouldn't eat anything more. "Poor thing. She won't let me stroke her and seems afraid even to let me touch her. We can't make a pet of her, children. I'll have to put her outdoors."

At this Arabelle ran down the stairs, into the basement and hid.

Nobody could find the little gray cat in the clutter.

At last Mrs. Foley said, "Time for bed." She shut the door between the basement and the kitchen.

The children went upstairs. Walt took his shower first.

The safest place for the ring was on Charlotte's finger. When it was her turn, she decided to wear it even in the shower.

Afterward Charlotte went down the hall to Walt's room at the back of the house. His light was out. Walt must already be asleep, she thought. Charlotte had wanted to talk to him.

She went back to her own room. After a while her mother came to say good night. But Charlotte lay awake for a long time.

She heard the sound of her parents getting ready for bed, and then the house was quiet.

Charlotte was still wearing the magic ring. It glowed with a faint blue light that seemed to be keeping her awake.

She put her hand under the pillow. Now she couldn't see the glow. But still she couldn't sleep. The house was full of strange creaking noises that night.

It sounded just as if someone were coming down the hall.

Both the children's rooms had windows overlooking the backyard. A full moon was starting to rise over the trees and rooftops. Soon Charlotte's room was white with moonlight.

The creaking was right outside her door now. Charlotte's mother had closed the door when she went out.

Charlotte heard the doorknob turn. She saw the door open.

Someone stepped into the room — someone too short to be her mother or father and much too tall to be Walt!

9

CHARLOTTE'S heart began to pound. She had never been so scared in all her life. She opened her mouth to scream, but she couldn't make a sound. She wanted to jump up and run down the hall to get her mother and father, but she couldn't move.

Charlotte had always thought she would be brave and clever if burglars came into the house. Now, when she had the chance, here she was, just shivering in her bed.

She clenched her fist under the pillow and felt the magic ring on her finger. It felt cool and somehow comforting. Charlotte felt better at once. She even began to feel brave again.

She decided to slide out of bed and

creep to the door. But Charlotte found she still couldn't move.

It must be the ring doing some of its magic, she told herself. She looked at the person who had come into her room.

A small woman in a long dress was standing in front of Charlotte's dresser. The moonlight made strange shadows, and Charlotte couldn't see the woman's face.

The woman looked at everything on the dresser top. She opened the box where Charlotte kept her seashell collection and picked up each shell in turn.

Then she opened a drawer and began to shake Charlotte's socks and underwear. At first she put the clothes back in the drawer, but after a while she started throwing things on the floor. She went into all the drawers.

She found the tin box where Charlotte kept the money she was saving to

buy birthday presents. The woman dumped the coins on the dresser top. She looked at each one, but she didn't take any of them.

Next she opened the closet and started to rummage through all the clothes hanging there. She seemed to be in a terrible hurry now. When a skirt or blouse slipped off a hanger, she just kicked it out of the way.

The woman kept looking around as if to be sure no one was watching her.

She must think I'm asleep, Charlotte said to herself. By now her room was a shambles. Charlotte wanted to yell, "You'd better pick up my clothes and clean up this mess," but she still couldn't make a sound.

At last the woman turned around and walked over to the bed. Now Charlotte could get a good look at her. In the moonlight she saw a sharp nose, a pointed chin, and shaggy hair.

It was the witch!

She must be after the magic ring hidden under Charlotte's pillow. But Charlotte was not going to let her have it!

10

Charlotte looked up into the woman's face. She knew she ought to be frightened, but the cool touch of the magic ring kept her calm and brave.

The witch just stood and stared down at the bed. She seemed to be looking right through Charlotte.

After a few moments the witch looked around the room. Then she scratched her head and walked out, leaving the door open. Charlotte saw her turn to go down the narrow hall to Walt's room. She must think he had the magic ring!

Charlotte wanted to protect her little brother. She tried to jump out of bed and chase after the witch, but she still could not move.

She lay in her bed and watched the open doorway.

All at once Charlotte saw a light. It

seemed to be coming from Walt's room. She thought she heard someone rush past her door and go downstairs.

Now the light came down the hall and into Charlotte's room. It was coming from a flashlight.

"Charlotte!" She heard her brother's voice. "Where are you?"

Charlotte found that she could wiggle her toes. She pulled her hand from under the pillow and sat up.

Walt blinked. "Where did you come from?"

"What do you mean?" Charlotte asked.

"You weren't here a second ago," Walt told her.

Charlotte caught sight of the ring. It was twinkling and jiggling as if it were laughing. She put her hand back under the pillow. She could still feel the ring shaking, but now she couldn't see it.

"You've done it again, Charlotte," Walt said. "I can't see you anywhere."

Charlotte kept her hand under the

pillow. "Can you hear me, Walt?"

"I can hear you," he said. "And I wish you'd tell me what's going on."

Charlotte kicked off the covers and looked at her feet.

She couldn't see them.

"I'm still in my bed," Charlotte said, "but I seem to be invisible."

Walt had seen the covers flying when his sister kicked them. "You're also spooky. Get visible!" He reached out and felt one of Charlotte's feet. He began to tickle it.

"Cut it out, Walt. We don't want to wake Mom and Dad." Charlotte pulled her hand with the ring from under the pillow.

Walt looked first at Charlotte and then at the ring. "We both have a lot to tell each other."

"Maybe you'd better tell your story first," Charlotte said. "I'm still trying to figure out what happened to me."

"I just saw the witch!" Walt said. "I was under the covers reading my library book with a flashlight. I guess she didn't see the light. Maybe she thought I was asleep. She pulled the covers down. I thought it was Mom, so I looked up right in her face."

"What did she do then?" Charlotte asked.

"She didn't do anything for a moment," Walt said. "Then, all of a sudden, she vanished."

11

WALT looked around Charlotte's bedroom. "I heard the witch run downstairs, so I came in here to tell you what happened to me. Besides, I didn't much feel like being alone just then."

Charlotte got out of bed and went to shut her door. "Do you think she's still in the house?" she whispered. "We ought to tell Mother and Daddy."

"They wouldn't believe us," Walt said. "And Mom will have a fit when she sees this room."

"The witch made this mess." Charlotte started to tell her brother how the witch had searched her room for the magic ring. While she talked, she picked up her clothes.

The ring on Charlotte's hand glowed softly. Almost before she finished telling how the room was messed up, the clothes were all back where they belonged.

Walt grinned. "That's another of the ring's neat tricks! What I want to know is how it makes you invisible."

"It seemed to happen when I put my hand under the pillow to hide the ring," Charlotte said.

Suddenly, both children heard the sound of the doorknob turning.

Walt turned off his flashlight and ducked into the clothes closet.

Charlotte jumped back into bed and tucked her hand with the ring on it under the pillow. She saw the door open. There was no light in the hall outside, and the moonlight had gone from the room.

Someone stepped into the room and snapped on the light.

It was Mrs. Foley. She looked at the bed. The covers were rumpled, but she couldn't see anybody there.

Mrs. Foley looked around. "Charlotte, Walt, where are you? I heard you talking just now."

Walt came out of the closet. His mother ran over to hug him.

As soon as Mrs. Foley turned away from her, Charlotte jumped out of bed. "Here I am, Mother."

"What were you two up to?" Mrs. Foley asked.

"We were hiding from a witch," Charlotte told her.

Mrs. Foley laughed. "This is no time for games, children." Then she was serious. "You really scared me. I thought something had happened to you. Please don't do it again. Now we'd all better get some sleep. I had the day off today, but tomorrow I have to go to work. We'll all have to get up early."

Mrs. Foley tucked Charlotte back into bed. She gave her a kiss and turned out the light.

She followed Walt down the hall to his room. There Mrs. Foley took the library book out of his bed and put it with his flashlight on the desk. "Go to sleep, Walt." Mrs. Foley kissed him. "You children will ruin your eyes by reading in bad light. It's no wonder you see witches in every shadow."

12

MR. Foley was already at the table when Charlotte came downstairs next morning. The blue plastic lid was on the floor near his chair. Arabelle was crunching away at something in the lid.

"This cat shared everything I had for breakfast," Mr. Foley said.

"What's she eating now?" Charlotte asked.

"Toasted English muffin, with jam," her father told her.

Walt walked into the dining room. "Arabelle has gotten fatter!"

Charlotte looked hard at the little cat. Walt was right. Arabelle was fatter, but she seemed changed in other ways, too. She must have washed herself. She looked much cleaner. She was almost fluffy. And the look on her face was different. Her eyes were round and playful now. And they didn't look nearly so green!

Arabelle finished the muffin and looked up at Mr. Foley.

"Do you want something else?" he asked.

The cat tipped her head to one side.

"You've had scrambled eggs, bacon, and a muffin. Maybe you'd like some coffee?" Mr. Foley poured a little black coffee into the lid.

Arabelle began to lap it up.

Mrs. Foley came in from the kitchen with a platter of bacon and eggs. Charlotte and Walt sat down at the table. Their mother filled a plate for each of them and one for herself. She caught sight of the cat.

"You look a lot happier this morning, Arabelle," Mrs. Foley said.

The cat licked the last drop of coffee from her whiskers.

"I see we won't have to rush out to buy cat food. You seem to like just about everything around here." Mrs. Foley dropped a slice of bread into the toaster.

"Then, may we keep her?" Charlotte asked. "Please, Mother?"

"We'll see," Mrs. Foley said. "She still won't let me pet her, but she's friendly now."

Mr. Foley looked up from his newspaper. "Here's a story about all the wild animals and birds that have come back to Prospect Park because the park department is letting a lot of things grow they used to cut down. There are even wild swans on the lake now."

"It's a beautiful day," Mrs. Foley told the children. "Why don't you have a picnic in the park?"

Neither Walt nor Charlotte said anything. After the magic that had happened yesterday, Prospect Park didn't seem very exciting.

Mr. and Mrs. Foley finished their breakfast and got ready to leave for work.

"Don't forget your key when you go out," Mrs. Foley reminded the children. "Bring the newspaper, Ed," she said to her husband. "We can read it on the subway."

13

"CHARLOTTE," Walt said, after their mother and father had left, "do you think the witch is still somewhere in the house?"

"Oh!" Charlotte had been so busy thinking about the cat, she had forgotten the witch. "I fell asleep last night and never heard her go out. Maybe she's right around here."

"She knows how to make herself disappear," Walt reminded his sister. "I feel creepy just thinking about it. Maybe we'd better go to the park after all."

Charlotte hated to admit that she was afraid to be in the house with the witch, but suddenly a picnic seemed like a great idea. She began to clear the breakfast dishes.

Almost before she started, Charlotte had the dishes in the dishwasher. Then she found the peanut butter, the jelly, and a loaf of bread. The sandwiches seemed to make themselves. They slid into the plastic sandwich bags.

Charlotte looked at the glowing ring. "How did I ever get along without you?"

Walt took four cans of lemon-lime soda out of the refrigerator. And Charlotte washed two big peaches.

Arabelle jumped on a chair so she could see what was going on. "Meow!"

"Sorry, Arabelle," Walt said. "Breakfast is over. This is for lunch."

The bicycles were kept in the basement. Walt and Charlotte took the bikes outdoors through the door under the front stoop. The cat followed them out of the house.

"Arabelle will be hungry and lonely if she stays out here," Charlotte said. "We don't want her to get all skinny and unfriendly again."

"We can't leave her in the house," Walt said. "She'd eat everything in sight."

Charlotte put an old doll's blanket in her wire handlebar basket. She leaned over to pick up the cat.

At once Arabelle moved away from the children. She stood watching them.

"Oh, I forgot! You don't like to be touched." Charlotte tucked a sandwich into the corner of the blanket. She held the bike steady. "I promise I won't touch you," she told the cat. "Come on, Arabelle, up you go!"

The cat checked the distance from the ground to the basket with her eyes. She put all four paws together and jumped. The jump was too high.

Charlotte tipped the bike so the cat landed in the basket on her way down.

"You're out of practice, Arabelle," Walt said.

There were two deep baskets, like saddlebags, on his bicycle. He put the cans of soda in one basket and the peaches and the rest of the sandwiches in the other.

Walt and Charlotte wheeled their bicycles into the street. They headed for Prospect Park.

14

ARABELLE sat in the basket on top of the doll's blanket. Her head was tipped back, and her tail stretched out behind her in the wind.

When Walt and Charlotte came to the park, they went through a big gate in the iron fence. It was summer. Except during rush hour, cars were not allowed in Prospect Park. People were roller-skating, jogging, and bicycling on the winding roads.

Walt and Charlotte rode along the stone path near the lake.

"Look, Charlotte! The swans are over by the little island." Walt jumped off his bicycle and wheeled it across the ground to the edge of the lake.

Charlotte followed him, wheeling her bike. The cat sat straight up in the basket, looking at everything with her big round eyes.

There were six swans. They all seemed the same size, but the mother and father birds were snowy white. The four young ones were brown and fuzzy.

"Come on, Charlotte. Let's ride around the park." Walt wheeled his bicycle back to the roadway.

"I'd like to let Arabelle see Lookout Mountain," Charlotte said. "It's too bad our bikes won't go up those steep paths."

Walt was riding in front of Charlotte. All at once she saw him grab hold tight to his handlebars. "Charlotte, my brakes aren't working!"

Charlotte was about to say, "Neither are mine!" but she caught herself just in time. "Hang on, Walt," she yelled. "The ring is playing tricks!"

The bicycles rolled along. Arabelle rode in her basket, turning to look at the joggers and skaters as they passed and enjoying the breeze through her whiskers.

At the hill called Lookout Mountain, they left the road and started up a rough woodland path.

The ride was smoother than ever.

"Walt," Charlotte called, "your wheels aren't touching the ground!"

He turned to look back at her. "Guess what? We're *flying!*"

15

LOOKOUT Mountain was much more overgrown than Charlotte and Walt remembered. This must be what the newspaper meant about the park department letting things grow that were usually cut down. Charlotte wished they hadn't let the poison ivy grow. There were huge clumps of it now.

The bicycles rose higher. They flew far above the poison ivy and swooped around the twisted old trees.

Charlotte and Walt looked down. It was spooky in the woods. Only a little light flickered through the tangled branches.

There were no other people here. The bicycles floated silently, high above the narrow path.

"The newspaper said wild animals

are coming back into the park," Walt said.

Charlotte pointed to a squirrel clinging head downward to a tree trunk.

A robin hopped across the path.

Next the children heard a twittering. A flock of purple finches flew down to peck at a fallen log.

Charlotte remembered the cat. How could she stop Arabelle from catching the birds? Charlotte had given her promise to the cat that she wouldn't touch her!

But Arabelle just sat in the bicycle basket and looked at everything around her. Not even the tip of her tail twitched.

"Caw! Caw! Caw!" A raven landed on the branch of a tree and stared at the children and the cat.

Charlotte leaned back and tipped up her front wheels. She began to pedal. The bicycle flew up through the treetops

into the blue sky. She turned to see that her brother was pedaling hard behind her.

The raven had come up out of the woods below. The bird flapped in wide circles high over the bicycles, as if to keep track of them.

Far below Walt and Charlotte could see the Long Meadow. People were playing baseball, flying kites, and throwing Frisbees.

No one seemed to be paying any attention to the bicycles in the sky, except the raven.

16

FLYING didn't seem to bother Arabelle at all. She sat in the bicycle basket and let the wind ruffle her soft gray fur. Her eyes were shining, and she looked as if she were having the time of her life.

Charlotte longed to stroke the little cat, but she remembered her promise and steered with both hands.

Walt followed Charlotte. The two bicycles zigzagged back and forth over the park. Suddenly Walt pedaled alongside his sister. He pointed at the ground. "Look at the stream!"

Charlotte held tight to her handlebars and craned her neck to look down.

She remembered the rocky stream trickling through the park last summer when there wasn't much rain. Now it was quite different.

The water rushed and gurgled from one small pool to another as it flowed between tree-covered hills. At last the stream came to a steep bank. Here it tumbled over large rocks in a foaming waterfall which splashed into the big lake in the park.

"How's that for a picnic place?" Walt said.

"Great!" Charlotte leaned forward to point her bicycle down.

It didn't seem a good idea to pedal among the kites and Frisbees. Charlotte flew over to the woods. Walt came after her. They coasted onto the rough ground near the stream.

Arabelle leaped out of the bicycle basket and ran to sit on a stone at the water's edge. She leaned over to look down into the stream.

The water was fast and bubbly on the other bank. Here beside the stone

it formed a quiet little pool. The cat could see herself as in a mirror.

Arabelle seemed to like what she saw. She jumped off the stone, chased a dragonfly, and made a running jump that landed her four feet up a tree.

"I'm glad Arabelle can get excited about something besides food." Walt began to take the sandwiches out of his bicycle basket.

Charlotte helped him set up a picnic place on a flat rock. She took Arabelle's sandwich out of its plastic bag and set it on a paper napkin on a rock a little distance away.

When Charlotte cut a slice from one of the big peaches to put it on the napkin, the seed fell out.

Charlotte saw that the outer shell of the peach seed was split in the middle. She took out the little kernel. "Too bad it doesn't taste like an almond," she said. "It looks just like one."

"What are you doing?" Walt asked.

Charlotte put the two peach seed halves side by side on the rock with the smooth inner hollows facing up. She filled them with lemon-lime soda. "I was wondering what Arabelle was going to use for a cup," she said.

17

THE peanut-butter-and-jelly sandwiches were the best they'd ever had. Arabelle had trouble at first trying to eat her slice of peach. It kept sliding away. She finally held it with both paws while she nibbled it. The cat liked the soda so much that Charlotte had to fill the twin peach seed cups six times.

When she had finished her meal, Arabelle washed her whiskers and then the rest of her face. She began to clean herself all over.

Walt and Charlotte finished eating. They gathered all the trash from their picnic and dropped it into a big park wastebasket.

The sun was warm. The children took off their socks and sneakers and left them on a rock. Then they rolled up their jeans and went wading in the cool stream.

Arabelle dipped one paw into the water. She pulled it out at once and shook it.

Charlotte laughed. "Arabelle, you act as if nobody ever taught you that cats hate to get wet."

Suddenly Walt grabbed his sister's arm. He pointed to the bicycles they had left leaning against a tree. Two big boys were getting ready to roll the bikes out onto the path.

"Stop!" Walt yelled. "Leave our bikes alone!"

"Make me!" jeered a short, thick boy with heavy boots.

Before Charlotte could stop him, Walt slipped the magic ring off her finger. He put it on and stepped out of the stream.

The ring began to sparkle. Walt was

barefoot, but he ran to the bicycles so fast that Charlotte could hardly believe her eyes.

The boy turned to look.

Wham! Walt ran right into him. The short, thick boy fell backward, and Walt slammed into the other boy.

This one was tall and strong. He got a grip on Walt's arm and tried to twist it. The ring was shooting sparks now. Walt pulled his arm free and punched

the boy so hard that he bounced right over the bicycles and crashed against the tree behind him.

Walt swung around. The heavy boy with the boots was walking away as fast as he could.

Charlotte came racing up. She grabbed hold of both bicycles. "You were brave, Walt," she told her brother. "I didn't know what to do."

The tall boy was sitting with his back against the tree.

"Are you hurt?" Charlotte asked him. "My brother doesn't know his own strength."

The boy just looked at her and at Walt. He stood up. "It's okay," he said. "I shouldn't have messed with your bikes." He walked away in a different direction from the boy with the boots.

18

"THAT was fun." Walt looked at the ring on his finger. A moment before it had been shooting sparks. Now it hardly shone at all. "I guess I'll hang onto this. It might come in very handy."

"I thought you said it wasn't a boy's ring," Charlotte said. She was afraid her brother wanted to use the magic ring just to win fistfights. "You *gave* it to me. And you kept telling me to get rid of it. Come on, Walt. Give it back!"

"Ow! It's burning me!" Walt yanked off the ring. He threw it on the ground.

Charlotte ran to pick it up.

Before she could reach the ring, a big black bird swooped down, grabbed it in its claws, and flew high up into a tall pine tree.

"Meow!" Arabelle raced over to the

pine tree and started to climb it.

Charlotte and Walt stood and looked up into the tree. For a little while neither of them said anything.

At last, Walt spoke. "I'm sorry," he said. "It's all my fault we lost the ring."

"Maybe it isn't lost." Charlotte went to put on her shoes and socks.

Walt followed her. "What do you mean?"

"Didn't you see the big nest in the top of that tree?" Charlotte asked.

"It's so big I couldn't miss it," her brother told her.

"I once read that crows and some other birds like to collect shiny things. They keep them in their nests. That raven has been following us. He was just looking for a chance to grab the ring."

Walt and Charlotte had their shoes and socks on now. They went back to the tree.

"You'd better stay with the bikes, Walt," Charlotte said. "I'm going to look in that nest."

"This is a *pine* tree, Charlotte," Walt reminded his sister. "The branches might break under you."

"I know, but it's a chance I have to take." Charlotte pulled herself up onto the bottom branch and began to climb the tree.

The lower branches were thick.

Charlotte stayed close to the trunk and held onto it with both hands. Up and up she went. She was afraid she'd get dizzy if she looked down, so she just kept climbing.

After a while the branches became thinner. Sunlight came down through the pine needles. Charlotte looked up. She could see the big untidy nest in a crotch of the tree. It was just out of reach above her head.

A little ball of soft gray fur was clinging to the edge of the nest.

Charlotte remembered Arabelle. She must have climbed up to the raven's nest, too.

The cat held something in her teeth, something small and blue that glittered in the sunlight. At first Charlotte couldn't believe her eyes. She just stared. But there was no doubt about it. Arabelle had found the magic ring!

19

CHARLOTTE thought for a few moments. The raven must have left the magic ring in the nest. Arabelle had climbed up and taken it. But why would the cat want the ring? Cats didn't collect shiny things.

Now Charlotte saw the raven. It was flying back. The bird was much bigger than Arabelle! It was going to attack her!

Charlotte climbed up toward the old nest, but the raven reached it first.

The dark shadow of the bird fell across the cat. Charlotte saw Arabelle look up at the cruel beak of the raven, aimed right at her face. The cat was so startled that she lost her grip and fell off the side of the nest.

Charlotte reached up and caught Arabelle in her arms.

The next minute she felt as if someone had caught her!

An arm held her steady until she could get her balance. When Charlotte had both hands on the tree trunk, she looked around for Arabelle. She couldn't see the little cat anywhere. A small woman in a black dress was standing beside her on the tree branch.

Charlotte was afraid the branch would crack under the weight of two people. She stepped onto the branch below. "Arabelle!" she called.

The woman on the branch overhead said something in a scratchy voice, but Charlotte went on calling, "Arabelle! Arabelle! Here kitty, kitty, kitty!"

She called and called. There was no sign of the cat. The woman in the black dress kept trying to tell her something, but Charlotte could think only of the cat.

Arabelle must have slipped out of her arms, Charlotte decided. She was sure she had caught her. That would have slowed Arabelle's fall. And cats were known to have nine lives!

Charlotte began climbing down the tree as fast as she could. The woman came down after her. She was old and stiff. It was hard for her to get down from one branch to the next. "Wait for me!" she rasped in her husky voice, but Charlotte was so upset about the cat that she didn't hear.

Charlotte looked on every branch of the tree for Arabelle. She didn't find her. At last she reached the ground.

Walt was waiting under the tree with

the bicycles. "What's all the noise about, Charlotte? Did Arabelle run away?"

Charlotte was out of breath. "Arabelle fell from the top of the tree!" she gasped. "I *know* I caught her, but something happened, and I can't find her anywhere."

"She must be stuck in the branches," Walt said. "I'll go look for her."

Before he could start up the tree, the woman in black came backing down from it. "You'll never see that cat again," she rasped. "And it's your own fault!"

20

CHARLOTTE had been trying not to cry, but now a big tear rolled down her cheek. "What do you mean?"

The woman turned around. The two children looked up into the craggy face of the witch.

For a moment neither of them spoke. Then Walt said, "What did we do to Arabelle?"

The witch's eyes filled with tears. She hid her face in her hands and sobbed.

"Was she your cat?" Charlotte asked.

The witch stopped crying. "Not exactly."

"But what was it we did?" Walt demanded.

"Charlotte touched me after she promised not to," the witch told him. "She broke the spell. Now I can't ever be a cat again. I have to stay like this." A tear trickled slowly down her long, sharp nose.

"You mean *you* are Arabelle?" Charlotte said.

The witch nodded. "I never had so much fun in my life as I did with you today. I really liked being a cat."

"And I liked having you for a cat, Arabelle," Charlotte said. "I'm sorry I touched you, but you were falling from a very tall tree. I thought you'd be hurt."

Arabelle rubbed her sharp chin. "Never mind, Charlotte. I'm blaming you because I hate to admit it was really my fault. If I were any good as a witch, I'd have been able to outsmart that raven. But I never was any good as a witch." She began to sniffle again.

Walt was staring at the magic ring that flickered dimly on the witch's hand.

"You did all right," he said. "You got what you were after, and you made fools of all the rest of us."

"If you wanted the ring so much," Charlotte said, "why didn't you get it out of the Fun Chicken yourself?"

"I tried," the witch said, "but the ring didn't want to come to me. Anyway, it's nobody's slave. It can be a friend, but you can't give it orders. I was hoping it would help me climb down the tree just now, but it didn't."

"Tell us about the ring," Walt said. "Where does it come from?"

"Nobody knows for sure," Arabelle told him. "It's very old, and is supposed to have belonged to Cleopatra and King Arthur and all sorts of other famous people. I spent years looking for it.

"Then I heard that it had been hidden in the Fun Chicken. I went to a lot of trouble to enchant a quarter that could get it out of there."

"Was that the quarter I used in the machine?" Walt asked.

The witch grinned. "Of course!"

"I thought you said it wasn't yours," Walt said.

"Charlotte asked if I'd lost a quarter," Arabelle reminded him. "I didn't lose it. I rolled it to you, hoping you could get the ring out of the box. What I didn't know was that the ring was just *waiting* for you two to come along." She pulled the ring off her hand and gave it to Charlotte. "You'll never believe me, but I climbed that tree just to get it for you!"

Charlotte slipped the ring on her finger. At once it started to twinkle.

21

A SMALL tree grew near the edge of the stream. The long trailing branches almost came down to the ground. They made a leafy green cave around the tree trunk.

Charlotte thought this was a good place to put the bicycles while they were wading in the stream. "Arabelle can go wading, too, now that she's not a cat."

The witch sat on the mossy ground in the tree-cave to take off her thick stockings and clumsy shoes. "It's a long time since I've gone wading. Nobody else I know does it."

Walt and Charlotte started to take off their socks and sneakers.

"There must be lots of things that are fun that only a witch can do, like flying on a broom," Walt said.

"That *was* fun," Arabelle admitted. "But I won't be able to do it now that I've broken the rules."

Walt stared at her. "Rules? I thought witches could do just about anything they wanted to."

The witch looked shocked. "That just shows what nonsense people believe. To practice witchcraft you must obey the rules, or you lose all your magic powers."

"What did you do wrong, Arabelle?" Charlotte asked her.

The witch grinned. "Just about everything," she said. "And I'd do it again if I had the chance. I had such fun! Witches must never eat the same food as ordinary people. But I don't enjoy stewed beetles' whiskers and crunchy bats' wings. I knew I shouldn't eat that corned-beef hash, but I was so hungry."

Arabelle stopped talking. She seemed to be thinking hard.

"What's the matter?" Walt wanted to know.

The witch stood up and stretched. "I've been wondering why I was so starved then. I just figured it out."

"Well?" Walt persisted. "What made you so hungry?"

Arabelle laughed. "The magic ring, of course. Charlotte was wearing it when she gave me the food. I've often heard that the ring loves to play tricks on witches."

"Then why would you want it?" Walt asked.

Arabelle didn't answer right away. Then she said, "I can't tell you that."

She thought for a minute. "I told you I'm not good as a witch. About all I could really do well was change myself into a cat, but even that power would be lost if I let anyone touch me. I was told never to become fond of ordinary people and taught that witches can't cry real tears."

"But you were crying just a little while ago," Walt said.

Arabelle nodded. "I knew then I'd really lost my powers."

The witch tucked up her long skirt in her wide belt and stepped out of the shadowy tree-cave into the bright sunshine.

The children followed her to the bank of the stream. Then the three of them stepped into the rushing water.

Arabelle's bare feet slipped on the pebbles under them. Both children

grabbed hold of the witch to keep her from falling.

Arabelle smiled. "All the while I've been longing for you to touch me," she said. "And I never knew it!"

22

SOON the witch was wading in the stream. She splashed among the rocks. "This is fun, now that I've got the hang of it!"

Charlotte and Walt found a small frog peeking out of a hole in the bank. They stood very still so as not to scare him. When Arabelle came over to see what was going on, the frog jumped into the water.

The witch laughed. "He's afraid I'll add him to a pot of brew along with shredded angleworms. He doesn't know I'd much rather have a cracker with peanut butter! Is there anything left from lunch, Walt? I'm beginning to get hungry."

"We ate everything we brought," Walt said.

Charlotte climbed out of the stream. "Let's put our shoes on and go home to get a snack."

Walt and Arabelle followed her to the leafy cave where they had left the bicycles. The children were back in their socks and sneakers before Arabelle had struggled into her thick black stockings and the shoes with brass buckles on them.

Charlotte wheeled her bicycle out into the sunshine. Walt came after her with his bike, and Arabelle followed him.

The witch was very quiet.

"What's the matter, Arabelle?" Charlotte asked.

"I'm too big to ride in your bicycle basket now," Arabelle said.

"All three of us will walk," Walt told her. "Charlotte and I can wheel the bikes home."

"That's nice of you," the witch said, "but I can't go home with you. Your mother won't want me for a pet now."

The children could see a tear in the corner of her eye, but they had no answer to this. They knew the witch was right.

"Where will you live?" Charlotte asked.

Arabelle looked around. "It's such a big park. There must be lots of places where I could stay."

"We could dig a cave in the side of Lookout Mountain," Walt said. "Nobody goes there anymore. You'd have the place to yourself."

"I don't dare go near poison ivy," Arabelle told him. "I'd like to live on that island with the swans. A friend of mine used to turn herself into a black

swan when she was in the mood."

Charlotte started walking along the stream, wheeling her bike. Walt and Arabelle came after her.

The ground was rough and stony, but the bicycles seemed to glide along. Charlotte had to hang onto her bike to keep it from going faster than she could walk. She felt the ring on her finger jiggle and saw it start to flash. It must

be laughing at her. What mischief was it up to now?

Charlotte looked behind her. Both Walt and Arabelle were trying to hold back his bicycle.

They came to the waterfall where the stream tumbled into the lake. The two bicycles lurched forward over the top of the steep bank. They dived down over the big rocks into the lake, dragging the children and Arabelle after them.

23

SIDE by side the bicycles splashed into the lake. Charlotte shut her eyes.

Walt was right. Magic was dangerous! How could Charlotte have trusted the ring? She felt herself thrown forward. Her feet seemed to land on the bicycle pedals.

Charlotte opened her eyes. Arabelle and Walt were sitting in a boat near her. Charlotte was in a boat, too. The bicycles had been turned into pedal boats like the ones for rent at the lake boat house!

The ring was sparkling for joy.

Charlotte was ashamed of herself for doubting the magic ring.

Walt was blinking and looking around.

Arabelle clapped her hands. "I always wanted to go for a boat ride, but witches are forbidden to cross water."

"Good old ring! This makes it much

easier to get to the island." Walt started to pedal his boat.

Charlotte followed. They went past the boat house and around the bend of the shore. Now they could see the little island.

It was surrounded by tall reeds growing in the swampy ground at the water's edge. Charlotte and Walt tried to get close to the shore, but their boats got stuck in the marsh.

Arabelle already had her shoes and

stockings off. She climbed out of the boat and waded through the reeds to the island.

The children hung their sneakers around their necks and stuffed their socks into the pockets of their jeans.

They climbed out of the pedal boats. Charlotte's feet were on the marshy ground first. She was still holding onto the side of her boat. Before she could let go, the ring flashed, and the boat vanished.

Another flash! Walt's boat was gone, too. "Now what do we do?" he asked.

Charlotte took a look at something in her hand. "Just be sure you put your bike away in a safe place," she told her brother.

Walt looked at the little bicycle he was holding. He grinned. "I was wondering how we'd get those boats out of the mud."

They began to wade to the island.

"Pick some reeds while you're out there," they heard a raspy voice call. "I need them for the house I'm building."

Charlotte and Walt picked as many reeds as they could carry. They found Arabelle working away in the middle of the tree-covered island.

"I lived in a reed house in Africa at one time," the witch said. "It was very cozy."

She had set sticks upright in a circle and tied the tops of them together. Now she wove the reeds between the sticks to make something like a big basket.

Arabelle looked at her work. "We've come to the part that's the most fun."

"What's that?" Walt asked.

The witch beamed. "The mud, of course!"

24

CHARLOTTE and Walt helped Arabelle gather mud from the shore of the island. They used it like plaster to cover the outside of the reeds that the witch had woven together.

"I'd forgotten how much fun it is to play with mud." Charlotte patted the side of the little house. "This is beginning to look like a chocolate igloo."

Walt added more mud and smoothed it with his hands. "What happens when it rains, Arabelle? Won't this all wash off?"

"It will if we don't waterproof it." The witch picked a large green leaf from a low branch. "Before the mud dries we

have to shingle the house with these."

This was much harder to do. All three of them worked carefully to anchor the leaves in the mud and make them overlap each other. When they had finished, the little house looked like a mound of green leaves. There was a door in one side, but no windows.

"Isn't it beautiful?" Arabelle backed into the little hut. "And it's just the right size for me." She poked her head out. "There isn't room for all of us at once, but we can enjoy it one at a time." She crawled out again. "Your turn now, Walt."

Walt and Charlotte each inspected the inside of the reed house. Charlotte thought it needed a carpet. They found patches of thick gray moss and covered the floor with it.

At last the little house seemed complete. They were all proud of it.

Walt started rubbing the mud off his hands onto the seat of his pants.

Charlotte looked down at her own dirty jeans. "I don't think Mother will let us come back after supper, Arabelle," she said. "We'll come tomorrow and bring you something to eat."

"You don't have to do that, Charlotte. I'm sure there are lots of bats around here." Arabelle's thin mouth cracked into a grin. "But I'd much rather have a peanut butter sandwich. I'll look for you tomorrow."

Walt placed his tiny bicycle on the ground. "How do we get our bikes back to the right size?"

Charlotte put her bicycle beside Walt's. The ring flashed twice, and the bikes were as big as usual.

The children pedaled up through the treetops. They waved to Arabelle. The

witch stood next to her little house and waved back.

The bicycles flew so high that nobody on the streets below could be sure what they were. There weren't any people outdoors on the block were Walt and Charlotte lived. They landed on the sidewalk in front of their house.

Charlotte used her key to unlock the front door. Her mother was in the kitchen.

Mrs. Foley went down to the basement and opened the door under the stoop. She helped the children bring the bicycles inside. "I can't find Arabelle," she said. "I'm afraid she has run away."

25

AT supper Mr. Foley said, "It's funny how much I miss that cat. Are you sure she's not around here somewhere? Did you look in the yard? And what about the furnace room?"

"I looked everywhere," Mrs. Foley told him. "And I called and called. Let's not talk about it anymore."

They didn't talk about the cat, but Charlotte saw that both her parents seemed sad. Nobody was very hungry.

Charlotte looked at the ring. The little lights in the deep blue circle were so dim now that she could hardly see them.

Next morning, after Mr. and Mrs. Foley left for work, Walt made a big pile of peanut butter sandwiches. "This ought to fill Arabelle up."

The children loaded their bicycle baskets with bananas and cans of soda, along with the sandwiches.

Charlotte couldn't make the bicycles fly. "This ring," she told her brother, "still only does what it wants to."

When they reached the park, Walt and Charlotte wheeled their bicycles along the stone wall by the lake till there was only a narrow marshy strip of water between them and the island.

"Please, Magic Ring," Charlotte begged, "make the bikes fly, so we can go over to see Arabelle."

There was not even a glimmer from the ring.

"Maybe it wants to make the bikes tiny. Then we could put them in our pockets and wade over to the island," Walt said. "How about it, Ring?"

The bicycles stayed their usual size.

"If we call Arabelle, she can wade

over to us," Charlotte said. She began to yell, "Yoo-hoo, Arabelle!"

No answer.

Walt called as loud as he could. After that the children took turns. Then they tried calling at the same time.

Still there was no answer.

"We have to get over to the island," Charlotte said, "but we'd better put the bikes in a safe place first."

They bicycled along the road to the Long Meadow, and followed the curving walks that led to the stream. Then they hid the bikes under the trailing branches of the little tree near their picnic place.

The two children raced as fast as they could around the shore of the lake. When they were close to the island, they waded across the marsh and pushed their way through the bushes on the bank to the reed house.

"I don't remember that the ground

was all trampled like this," Walt said.

"It wasn't," Charlotte told him. "Look, Walt!" She pointed to something that was snagged on a tree root.

"That's Arabelle's shoe!" Walt ran to the little hut. "The other one is in here." Walt stepped inside the reed house.

Charlotte went over and looked into the hut. She couldn't see her brother. Charlotte couldn't understand it. There was nowhere in the little house to hide!

She had to bend down to go through the doorway, but once inside there seemed to be lots of room overhead. A soft light came from somewhere far behind her. And all around were feathery gray-green trees!

Charlotte's eyes were getting used to the dim light. Now she saw her

brother. He was staring up at the trees.

"Walt," Charlotte whispered.

"What is this?" he asked. "More magic?"

Charlotte nodded.

The ring was glowing softly.

Charlotte looked around at the strange forest. A newly trampled path led through the trees. She saw a scrap of black cloth that was caught on a low branch.

"That's a piece of Arabelle's dress!" Charlotte said.

Walt began to march quickly down the path. Charlotte hurried after him.

26

CHARLOTTE and Walt followed the narrow path between the trees. The light became even dimmer as they went along.

The path was sprinkled with chunks of pale dirt in which they could see many strange footprints. The path went up a hill of dirt. At the top the children came to a hole. The footprints went down into it.

Charlotte picked up another shred of black cloth from the ground. "They've taken Arabelle in here!"

Walt stepped into the dark hole and started down the steep path.

When Charlotte followed him, the ring on her finger shone brighter. It lit up the darkness around the two children with a soft blue light.

The path became a winding passage that went past dark, cavelike rooms where strange animals lurked. Some of them looked as big as horses. Long thin horns swayed on their heads, and they seemed to have more than four horrible, skinny legs.

One of them stood in a shadowy curve of the passage. Walt held his breath, and Charlotte tried not to shudder as they passed it.

A flickering red glow lit up the passage ahead of them. They could hear angry voices. As they walked, the light became brighter, and the voices were louder.

The two children could almost make out what was being said.

Walt turned to look at Charlotte.

"Yipe! There's no hope of you hiding from whomever has hold of Arabelle! The ring is like a spotlight."

Charlotte shoved her left hand deep into her jeans pocket to hide the ring. She followed Walt toward the ruddy glow ahead.

Now they could hear Arabelle's raspy voice. Someone answered her in a high-pitched shriek.

Walt and Charlotte had come to the end of the passage. They peeked into a large room. It was lit only by the fire under an iron pot.

Arabelle was standing between two women in long blue dresses. They had frizzy hair and pointed hats, and had tight hold of both Arabelle's arms. Facing her was a strong-looking woman with mean little eyes and stringy black hair. She was wearing a dark purple dress and hat. Nearby were nine other women, all in different colors, and all with pointed hats.

Charlotte and Walt were in a den of witches!

The purple witch was talking again. "You've had your last chance, Arabelle. I thought you learned your lesson when we took away your hat and made you wear black. You know your orders were to get that ring and give it to me! You had it right in your hand and you gave it to two ordinary children!"

Arabelle pulled her arms free and stepped forward. She was barefoot and tattered, but she stood on tiptoe and stared into the mean little eyes. "Hedwig," she said. "The ring was meant for Walt and Charlotte, not for me or for you. I'm *glad* I gave it to them!"

27

HEDWIG glared down at the little witch. "You won't be glad you disobeyed me when I have finished with you, Arabelle. From now on you will do the dirty work, keep the brew boiling, frost the bats' wings, wash the animals, and care for my pet spider."

"Shan't!" Arabelle said.

The purple witch raised her thick arm to hit her. Arabelle dodged out of the way.

"Witches!" Hedwig shrieked, "as your leader, I command you to take hold of her!"

All the witches in their many-colored hats and dresses crowded around ragged little Arabelle and pinned her arms to her sides.

The head witch came toward Arabelle with her fists clenched.

"I've had enough of this!" Walt charged across the room with his head down like a billy goat. He rammed Hedwig in the stomach. She let out a roar and reached for him.

Charlotte wasn't going to let anybody hurt her brother. She raced over to the head witch. Her left hand was jammed into her pocket. Charlotte knocked the witch's hat off with her right hand.

Hedwig whirled around. She didn't seem to know what had happened.

But Walt knew! He jumped clear of the witch and knocked off the hats of two of her helpers. "Charlotte!" he yelled. "You've done it again!"

For a second she didn't know what he was talking about. Then Charlotte held up her right hand. She couldn't see it. She looked down. She couldn't see the rest of herself, either. And neither could anyone else!

Now Charlotte ran to help Walt grab the other witches' hats. They threw the hats back and forth between them. The witches wailed in fury. They tried to rescue their hats from Walt, but just as they were about to grab them, Charlotte would carry them off.

Charlotte stacked the hats one inside the other and put the stack of hats on Arabelle's shaggy head. "You look lovely, Arabelle," she whispered.

Arabelle began to dance around the room.

Hedwig frowned. Suddenly she roared, "Ants! Come forth! You were masters here until yesterday. Ants do not need eyes to find things. Fetch me this invisible pest, and I will give you back your underground castle!"

From all around the big room there was the sound of footsteps. Strange animals came out of the shadows into the firelight. They had six legs and long waving horns like the animals Charlotte and Walt had seen on their way through the narrow passage.

Now the children saw that these were giant ants. The horns were feelers that they could use like radar!

All the ants started racing straight toward Charlotte. Their feelers had told them just where she was!

28

ARABELLE took the stack of pointed hats off her head. She began to toss the hats over the feelers of the giant ants.

Walt ran to help her.

Soon the ants were bumping into each other and moving in circles. The witches ran around, trying to get their hats back.

In the excitement, an ant kicked over the iron pot. The fiery witch's brew flowed across the floor, and the big room began to fill with smoke. At once the ants rushed to save the young ants and ant eggs in the other rooms of the ant castle.

Charlotte pulled her left hand out of her pocket. Now she was visible. The ring glowed brightly on her finger, but everybody was so busy trying to escape from the fire and the smoke that nobody even noticed her.

Charlotte rushed over to Walt and Arabelle. "Let's get out of here!" She grabbed each one by the hand and dragged them both toward the winding passage.

As the three crossed the big room, they passed Hedwig. She was trying to get her purple hat out of the jaws of an ant who had decided to eat it. Charlotte pulled both Walt and Arabelle away before either one could say anything to the head witch.

The narrow hall was crowded with sobbing witches and scurrying ants. Charlotte kept tight hold of her brother and the ragged little witch. Her eyes were stinging from the smoke.

When Charlotte thought she could no longer stand it, the passage began to slant uphill. At last they climbed out of the hole and started running down the path between the feathery trees. The light became brighter as they ran.

Suddenly Charlotte was blinking in the bright sunlight. "What happened to the forest?" She looked around and saw that the three of them were standing with their backs to the doorway of the little reed house.

"There's your forest." Arabelle pointed to the soft, gray-green moss on the floor of the little hut.

Walt was thinking hard. "You must have built your house on an anthill! But how did we get so small? And how did you get down in there?"

"It was all Hedwig's doing," Arabelle said. "She kidnapped the Ant Queen. This gave her the power to make anybody in the ant kingdom ant-size. My house was built right on top of the ant kingdom, so she kidnapped me." Arabelle grinned. "Thanks for coming to the rescue!"

"We'll have to find another place to build a house," Walt said. "Right now we'd better go see if our bikes are all right. We hid them under the tree by the stream where we left them yesterday."

Arabelle pushed through the bushes on the island's edge and started wading through the marsh.

Walt and Charlotte took off their sneakers and socks and followed her.

29

WALT and Charlotte followed Arabelle around the shore of the lake until they came to the stream. They walked to the place where they had gone wading yesterday.

Walt ran over to the leafy tree-cave. "The bikes are safe and sound," he told his sister. "We'd better give Arabelle the sandwiches."

"Look!" Charlotte pointed.

Arabelle was washing herself as best she could without soap. When she had finished she went to sit in the sun. The witch was seated on the stone by the little mirrorlike pool. She bent over to look at her face in the water.

Charlotte and Walt waded over to where Arabelle was hunched over the quiet pool.

She was staring down at her battered old face. Arabelle seemed so unhappy that Charlotte couldn't bear it.

Without knowing why she did it, Charlotte slipped the magic ring off her finger and held it on top of Arabelle's shaggy gray hair.

The witch looked at herself in the water. She saw the ring get bigger and bigger.

As the ring became bigger, it became warmer. Soon it was too hot to hold. Charlotte had to let go of it!

The ring rested on Arabelle's hair for a moment, like a lovely crown. Then Walt and Charlotte saw the witch begin to shrink. In just a few seconds her head was so small that the ring slipped over it and rested on her shoulders.

Now the ring was getting smaller. It was like a collar around Arabelle's neck. The witch was still shrinking, but the sparkling collar shrank with her.

"Charlotte," Walt whispered, "I was afraid Arabelle was going to disappear altogether, but she seems to have stopped getting smaller. Only now she looks as if she needs a shave!"

The little witch was covered with so

much soft gray fur that Charlotte and Walt couldn't even see her clothes. Her ears were pointed, and her eyes were deep blue with little silvery flecks in them, just like the collar around her neck.

Charlotte couldn't say a word.

"Guess what? You're a cat again, Arabelle!" Walt said.

30

ARABELLE looked at herself in the quiet little pool. The little gray cat stretched. Then she leaped from the rock to the shore. She chased a tiny blue butterfly along the bank of the stream.

"I wonder what time it is," Charlotte said.

"My stomach tells me it's lunch-time," Walt told her. He stepped up onto the bank and began to take the sandwiches and soda out of his bicycle baskets.

They picnicked on a big rock beside the stream. "Arabelle won't need so many sandwiches now," Walt said. "There'll be enough for us, too."

When the last banana had been eaten, Arabelle curled up on the big rock to take a nap.

The children went back to splashing in the cool water. Charlotte found a green leaf floating on the stream. She pretended it was a boat.

Walt looked for a leaf he could use for a boat. Then they raced the leaves in the rushing stream.

After a while they decided to use sticks for boats. Before they had found just the right sticks, Arabelle woke up.

"Meow!"

"Don't tell me you're hungry again!" Walt said.

The cat bumped her head against his leg and purred.

Walt and Charlotte put on their sneakers and socks. Charlotte picked up the furry little cat and put her in her handlebar basket.

The children wheeled their bicycles out into the late afternoon sunshine. Walt and Charlotte could hear the sound of traffic in the park.

"It must be rush hour. Mother and Dad will be home already." Charlotte climbed on her bike.

"Too bad we don't have the ring any more," Walt said. "We'll have to buck the traffic." He got ready to pedal.

The cat's collar flashed, and the two bicycles floated up into the air. They flew high over the trees and the traffic and the Brooklyn houses.

"Who says we don't have the ring? Arabelle and the ring go together from now on!" Charlotte reached forward to scratch the little cat behind the ears.

The bicycles landed on a quiet street a block away from their house. Walt and Charlotte pedaled home.

Mrs. Foley was standing on the front stoop. "Oh, you found Arabelle!" She ran down the steps, picked up the furry little cat, and held her against her cheek. "We're having pot roast tonight, Arabelle. Is that all right with you?"

Arabelle purred.

Other books by Ruth Chew

The Wednesday Witch
Baked Beans for Breakfast
(also known as *The Secret Summer*)
No Such Thing as a Witch
Magic in the Park
What the Witch Left
The Hidden Cave
(in hardcover as *The Magic Cave*)
The Witch's Buttons
The Secret Tree House
The Would-Be Witch
Witch in the House
The Trouble With Magic
Summer Magic
Witch's Broom
The Witch's Garden
Earthstar Magic
The Wishing Tree
Second-hand Magic
Mostly Magic
The Magic Coin
The Witch at the Window
Trapped in Time
Do-It-Yourself Magic